AGENT P'S
TOP SECRET
JOKE BOOK

Written by Jim Bernstein and Scott Peterson
Based on the series created by Dan Povenmire & Jeff "Swampy" Marsh

Disney PRESS
New York

D0032574

DR. DOOFENSHMIRTZ

TOP SECRET

Greetings! You have been chosen to participate in a top secret mission. Here it is: the evil Dr. Doofenshmirtz has created his most diabolical invention yet—the De-Laugh-inator. With it, he plans to remove all laughter from the Tri-State Area. Obviously, that would make it a pretty dull place to live. We need your help to foil his plan. Read the jokes in this book and then tell them to your friends. The laughter that you produce should help defeat Dr. Doofenshmirtz. I only hope that we're not too late to stop him!

You will be assisting Agent P in this operation.

Before we can proceed with your training, you must swear this secret oath of allegiance to the Organization Without a Cool Acronym, also known as the OWCA. Please say the following oath out loud: **"O-Wah. Tah-Goo. Siam."** Now, say it faster. **"O-Wah-Tah-Goo-Siam."** Faster! **"O-Wah-Tah-Goo-Siam."** Faster! **"Owahtahgoosiam."** Ha-ha-ha! Made you say, "Oh, what a goose I am!" Congratulations, you are now an official agent of the OWCA.

Now that you've been sworn in, I can tell you a few jokes that we agents like to share around the watercooler.

What is a secret agent's favorite bug?

A spy-der.

How many secret agents does it take to change a lightbulb?

We can't tell you. It's a secret!

What do the FIRESIDE GIRLS stand for?

The Pledge of Allegiance.

Okay, let me tell you a little bit about the OWCA. Our agency consists of an elite team of animal agents whose mission is to protect the Tri-State Area from evildoers. Our most highly skilled operative is Agent P (also known as Perry the Platypus).

AGENT P

Agent P can be identified by his bluish green hue, his duck bill, and his very cool fedora-style hat. In fact, all of our agents wear fedoras. We don't remember when it started, but one of the agents began wearing a fedora and then everyone wanted to.

What did one fedora say to the other fedora?

You wait here. I'll go on *ahead*!

THIS IS OUR INTERN, CARL KARL, WHO APPARENTLY HAS A JOKE OR TWO HE WANTS TO TRY OUT. AND YES, THAT'S HIS REAL NAME. CLEVER, HUH?

CARL: What happens when you drop a grand piano on yourself, sir?

MAJOR MONOGRAM: What?

CARL: You get a *flat* major!

CARL: Major Monogram, sir, what's the difference between great kite-flying weather and our favorite platypus?

MAJOR MONOGRAM: I don't know, Carl.

CARL: One's a clear blue sky, and the other is our dear blue spy.

MAJOR MONOGRAM: Don't you have work to do, Carl?

Okay, Carl had to run out to get my lunch, so let's get back to Agent P. Agent P wants you to know that in order to defeat the evil Dr. Doofenshmirtz, you will have to tell jokes about anything and everything—even about Agent P himself!

What do you call a giant, flying, prehistoric platypus?

A *Perry*-dactyl.

What's the difference between an old, made-up story and a platypus appendage?

One's a fairy tale and the other's a *Perry tail*.

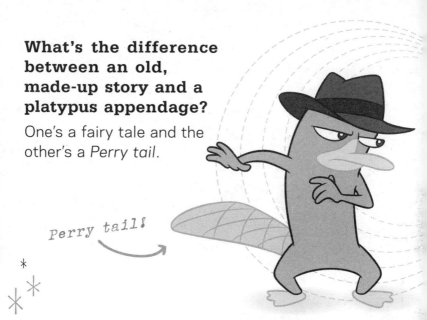

Perry tail!

What did Phineas and Ferb (more about them later!) wish their pet platypus on December twenty-fifth?

PERRY CHRISTMAS!

What follows Agent P wherever he goes?

His tail.

Why isn't Perry's bill twelve inches long?

Because then it would be a foot!

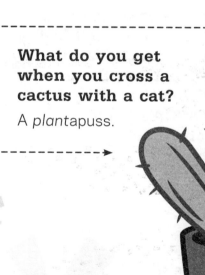

What do you get when you cross a cactus with a cat?

A *plant*apuss.

It's important that you can recognize other undercover agents in the field and that you know their specialties. Here are a few photos of some of our secret agents in the OWCA. But the riddles on the next few pages are about some of our *newest* secret agents. We haven't had time to take their pictures. Carl is still working on that. But these jokes will help you to identify some of the OWCA's brand-new members. Now get to work!

AGENT D

AGENT H

AGENT F

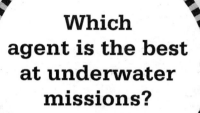

Which agent is the best at underwater missions?

Agent C.

WHICH AGENT IS THE BEST GOLFER?

Agent T.

WHICH AGENT EXCELS AT SURVEILLANCE?

Agent I.

In order to defeat Dr. Doofenshmirtz, you're going to have to know everything about him. Dr. Doofenshmirtz tries to wreak havoc with his evil inventions, or what he calls "-inators." The main cause of Dr. Doofenshmirtz's evil is his tragic childhood. For example, when he was a child, Dr. Doofenshmirtz's parents forced him to work as a lawn gnome. If I were Dr. Doofenshmirtz, I'd be very evil, too!

Why couldn't Dr. Doofenshmirtz go out and play?

He had to do his *gnome*work!

What does Dr. Doofenshmirtz call his latest invention to get rid of those in-line-skating restaurant servers he despises so much?

The Waiter-Skater-Hater-inator!

What did Dr. Doofenshmirtz yell at Agent P as he hit him with a pocketbook?

Purse you, Perry the Platypus!

What does Dr. Doofenshmirtz call the invention that will eventually make him ruler of the Tri-State Area?

His Sooner-or-Later-Dictator-inator.

What does Dr. Doofenshmirtz wear under his jackets?

Doofen-*shirts*.

What is Dr. Doofenshmirtz's favorite license plate?

I (HEART) N8ORS

Why wasn't Dr. Doofenshmirtz surprised when his robot messed up one of the doctor's evil plans?

Around his place, that's the *norm*.

- -

DR. DOOFENSHMIRTZ: Hey, Norm, I just invented something *very evil* that lets people see through walls!

NORM: What do you call it?

DR. DOOFENSHMIRTZ: A window!

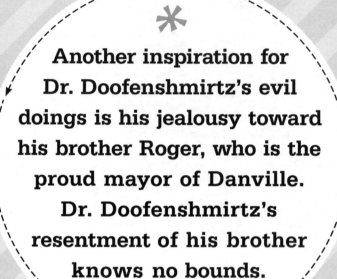

Another inspiration for Dr. Doofenshmirtz's evil doings is his jealousy toward his brother Roger, who is the proud mayor of Danville. Dr. Doofenshmirtz's resentment of his brother knows no bounds.

Now, I want you to look carefully at these two faces.

After you have memorized them, eat this book. Just kidding, don't eat the book. These two boys are **Phineas** and **Ferb.** When Agent P is undercover, they are his owners and best friends. They live in Danville with their parents and their older sister, Candace. In order to defeat Dr. Doofenshmirtz, you will have to tell some jokes about Phineas and Ferb. We added one joke about Agent P, so he wouldn't feel left out.

What runs all around Phineas and Ferb's backyard but never moves?

Their fence.

What do you get when you mix Phineas with basil?

Phineas and *herb*.

What did Phineas say when he saw his mom's broken lamp?

Ferb, I know what we're gonna *glue* today!

What did Phineas say when Ferb forgot to put out the milk for breakfast?

Hey, where's *dairy*?

HEY, FERB, WHY DID PERRY CROSS THE ROAD?

I HAVE NO IDEA.

BECAUSE THE CHICKEN HAD THE DAY OFF!

What's the one thing Phineas and Ferb have that Candace doesn't?

A sister.

In what month does Ferb talk the least?

February—it's the shortest!

HOW MANY DIFFERENT METHODS DID PHINEAS AND FERB CREATE TO INFLATE THEIR POOL THIS SUMMER?

104—BECAUSE THERE ARE 104 WAYS OF SUMMER INFLATION!

As I mentioned earlier, Phineas and Ferb live with their loving parents and sister, Candace. Normally, I don't like to make jokes about people's families, but we must do anything to stop Dr. Doofenshmirtz, no matter how horrible.

Why didn't Candace use her new spy camera to bust the boys?

It was busted!

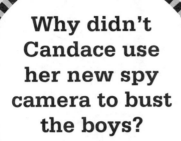

WHaT'S THE DIFFERENCE BETWEEN PHINEAS AND FERB'S MOM AND A FISHERMAN?

One's a Flynn-Fletcher, the other is a *fin-fetcher*.

What does Candace want her mom to do during spring-cleaning?

DUST HER BROTHERS!

WHAT DID MR. FLETCHER SAY TO THE BUTCHER?

Nice to *meat* you!

WHEN JEREMY INVITED CANDACE TO A HALLOWEEN PARTY, WHAT DID SHE WANT TO DRESS UP AS?

Jeremy's *ghoul*friend!

Some of the other civilians you may encounter in the area are the friends of the Flynn-Fletcher family. They know Agent P only as Perry the Platypus, but they are considered very friendly.

What does Isabella say when she wants to borrow a stick of gum?

Whatcha chewin'?

What's Jeremy's favorite French dance?

The Can-Can*dace*.

Why wouldn't Jeremy let his bandmate play a flounder instead of a guitar?

Because you can't tune a fish!

What does Buford call his favorite place to sit?

Baljeet.

IF IRVING COULD BE ANY OF THE THINGS PHINEAS AND FERB CAN BUILD, WHAT WOULD HE BE?

A fan!

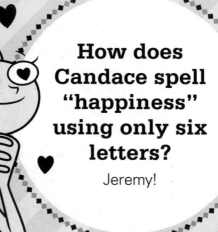

How does Candace spell "happiness" using only six letters?

Jeremy!

Once, two brothers named Thaddeus and Thor had a contest with Phineas and Ferb to see who could build a better clubhouse. Phineas and Ferb were crowned the winners. It's now your job to answer a joke about Thaddeus and Thor!

PHINEAS: Why was Thaddeus's brother angry?

FERB: Because he was a *Thor* loser.

Phineas and Ferb are remarkably good at building fantastic contraptions to make the most of every day. Knowing about their inventions may provide you with some jokes that will help you defeat Dr. Doofenshmirtz.

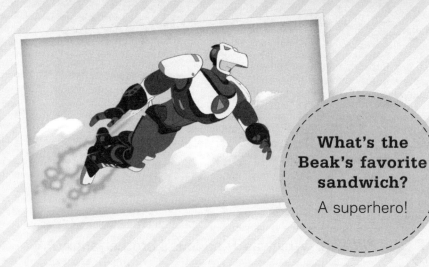

What's the Beak's favorite sandwich?

A superhero!

BALJEET: I just went golfing and I got a hole in one.

BUFORD: Don't worry. I'm sure they can fix it!

ISABELLA: Hey, Phineas, how do you like the new roller coaster you built?

PHINEAS: Oh, it has its ups and downs.

Why didn't Phineas and Ferb worry when Candace took their giant bowling ball?

Because they had a spare.

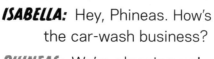

ISABELLA: Hey, Phineas. How's the car-wash business?

PHINEAS: We're cleaning up!

BALJEET: Now that your your car wash has closed, did you make a lot of cash?

PHINEAS: Nah, it was a wash.

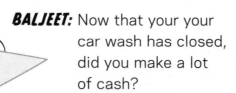

Why didn't the waiter charge Perry when he went to Chez Platypus?

He already *had* a bill!

How did the Phinedroid say good-bye to the Ferbot?

Oil be seeing you!

What's a Ferbot's favorite song?

Ro-ro-ro your *bot*, gently down the stream!

BUFORD: Why do you robots always think you're better than humans?

PHINEDROID: Well, we never need to eat, sleep, or use the bathroom.

BUFORD: *Pfff*. Those are my three favorite things to do!

FERB AND I JUST INVENTED A WATCH THAT CAN DO CALCULATIONS, CAN PREDICT WEATHER FORECASTS, AND IT CAN EVEN DO VIDEO CONFERENCING. ANY IDEA WHAT WE SHOULD CALL IT?

WATCH-A-DOIN?

Phineas: Hey, Ferb. What kind of dessert goes best with our antigravity machine?

Ferb: A *float*!

BALJEET: What is an alien's favorite type of song? A *nep*-tune.

BUFORD: I don't get it.

OH, I GET IT. A NEP-TUNE!

GOOD JOB, BUFORD.

Phineas and Ferb accidentally caused Meap's ship to crash while playing baseball with their remote-controlled baseball launcher. Now it's your turn to provide the answer to an important baseball-related joke.

CANDACE: What is a baseball player's favorite animal?

JEREMY: A bat!

Great Googlie Mooglie!

We've just received a report that Dr. Doofenshmirtz is about to fire his De-Laugh-inator! It's time to go into *EMERGENCY JOKE MODE!*

KNOCK-KNOCK.
WHO'S THERE?
FERB.
FERB WHO?
FERB PETE'S SAKE, LET ME IN ALREADY!

KNOCK-KNOCK.
WHO'S THERE?
CANDACE.
CANDACE WHO?
CANDACE BE THE RIGHT ADDRESS OR AM I LOST AGAIN?

KNOCK-KNOCK.
WHO'S THERE?
ISABELLA.
ISABELLA WHO?
IS A *BELL* A-RINGING? 'CAUSE I COULD'VE SWORN I KNOCKED.

KNOCK-KNOCK.
WHO'S THERE?
PHINEAS AND THE FERB-TONES.
PHINEAS AND THE FERB-TONES WHO?
SERIOUSLY, YOU'VE NEVER HEARD OF US? WE SANG "GITCHIE-GITCHIE GOO." WE WERE A ONE-HIT WONDER!

KNOCK-KNOCK.
WHO'S THERE?
CARL.
CARL WHO?
CARL A DOCTOR, YOU JUST SLAMMED
MY FOOT IN THE DOOR!

How could Major Monogram tell that Agent P was feeling sad?

Because he was a little *blue*.

What time is it when a platypus breaks through your wall?

Time to get a new wall!

Dr. Doofenshmirtz thinks he can break
Agent P's concentration with a joke.
LET'S SEE HOW IT GOES. . . .

DR. DOOFENSHMIRTZ: What's green and has four wheels?

DR. DOOFENSHMIRTZ: Grass. I lied about the wheels! Oh, Perry the Platypus, I truly crack myself up sometimes.

Perry was minding his own business, eating some potato chips, when all of a sudden one of them spoke to the other. What did the potato chip say to his friend?

Shall we go for a *dip*?

What's a platypus's favorite fruit?

Gr-rr-rr-apefruit.

YOU DID IT! The people of the Tri-State Area are laughing again. Dr. Doofenshmirtz's De-Laugh-inator has been destroyed!

CONGRATULATIONS! On behalf of the entire agency, I thank you. And now, Agent P would like to thank you personally.